In Denial

SHRADHA KHANNA

In Denial

SHRADHA KHANNA

KALAMOS LITERARY SERVICES LLP

Kalamos Literary Services LLP
Email: info@kalamos.co.in | editorial@kalamos.co.in
Published in 2021
by
Kalamos Literary Services
ISBN- 978-93-90909-06-3
Copyright © *In Denial 2021*
Shradha Khanna

Typeset in Kalamos Literary Services LLP

Cover designed by Brand Inspire OPC Pvt. Ltd.
Print and bound in India.

_To,_
All my readers out there.

1

The Encounter

It is that time of the year when the whole city is submerged in water, roads get flooded and it becomes difficult for people to drive without splattering water everywhere. Tonight too, it is pouring hard and I am sitting on a drenched bench with an umbrella in one hand and typing on my phone with the other. Even with an umbrella I am soaked to the toe, the feeling is liberating as I am finally taking the right decision in my life.

Sometimes, it takes a moment to realise and decide upon something. Sometimes, it takes days or even years to come upon a right decision. Two things matter a lot when taking the right decision, timing and realisation, for me both happened simultaneously. I realised in the nick of time, took the right decision and saved three lives from being ruined. Maybe if you decide to read along my story you would call me selfish, ironically it is exactly this word "Selfish" that helped me land upon the right decision.

My life was simple, planned and stagnant, in short boring, until that breezy co-incidence happened two months ago. I am still in shock or better yet call it a haze, but now that I have taken the decision I must stick to it, mustn't I? Sighing, I scrolled on to the number which turned my life inside out. Forced me to feel things, imagine things I never thought about. I am not even sure if what I am about to do will be in my favour but for the first time in my life I have no plan B. Believe me, it is as terrifying as a person suddenly taking his last breath, I feel helpless, uncertain and that is one emotion I have not felt since my mother's death. That was the most painful time of my life. My mom was diagnosed with a rare kind of cancer, her health digressed too fast before the doctors could even start with the chemotherapy. Dad says that mom is lucky because she passed away before she could suffer more, I disagree. If she had more time maybe we could have saved her.

I miss her every day. Every year on her birthday I visit this NGO for elderly people where mom used to volunteer once a month. If I dare put two & two together then I have a strong feeling that it was my mom's soul which saved me from making a blunder in my life. Mom always used to say that loving openly and sincerely can make your life magical and worth living.

Visiting the NGO two months earlier, on her birthday, changed my life completely.

Two months earlier

I got down from my car and picked the heavy carton of clothes which I am supposed to donate to this NGO. It's a small gesture which brings a little bit of peace to me and makes me feel closer to mom. Sonia who is the head of this NGO, knows me pretty well. I like her as she does not ask many questions and has never looked at me with sympathy. The NGO was on the way to my office, which was great as I have a meeting in another 30 minutes and I cannot afford to be late.

On entering the NGO's office, I could not find Sonia, instead I was welcomed by a cheerful girl and her name is …

"Hi, I am Vedika. Welcome to the Care House, how can I help you?"

"Umm I was looking for Ms Sonia?"

"Sonia di is out for some work, Can I do something for you?" smiling widely she asked. There is something about her being so cheerful that makes me uncomfortable standing here.

Picking up the carton, I put it on her desk and spoke, "These are clothes for the NGO, let Sonia know about it."

"Okay, and what's your name?"

"Ridwan, Sonia knows me and I scheduled an appointment with her for 10 am today." I replied.

Rolling her eyes, she pretended to look at the watch and then with a bored expression she said, "WOW, you are on time."

Before I could react, she told me to follow her. While matching her small steps I asked her, "Do you mind telling me where we are going?"

"Everyone is having breakfast or tea inside, it would be good time to meet them."

Stopping in my tracks, I uttered, "Hey I did not sign up for this, could you please call Sonia, she would explain."

Turning around, she replied, "What's there to ask, you brought things for them, you should know who you are donating to." Then a little too excited, she spoke, "Believe me, you would love meeting them."

I was still shaking my head when she gave me that pleading look and requested, "It would mean a lot to them." Hesitantly, I shook my head, still not comfortable with the idea but went along with her.

The moment we entered the room she greeted everyone with a loud cheer, which was not needed, then she diverted everyone's gaze towards me and gave them my introduction, it was embarrassing but I managed to smile. The whole meeting with everyone went on for 20 minutes before I had the opportunity to say goodbye. Relief washed over me when I exited the room, there were far too many people for my liking.

As I reached the main door Vedika called out from behind, was not aware that she was following me, "How was your experience meeting them?"

My first reaction was to tell her that I am relieved leaving that room but seeing her hopeful expression I said "it was okay."

Blinking, she repeated, "Okay…" I nodded.

Within a span of a few seconds, her expression turned remorseful and she said, "You went there to please me, you did not enjoy it there. Well, that was very selfish of you."

Her sentence bothered me. I turned to explain but she was not there. I was about to chase after her when my phone rang, picking up I spoke in an irritated tone. It was my secretary informing me of my meeting which was about to start in fifteen minutes. Thanking her, I decided to deal with Vedika next time and left for my car.

2

The Feelings

The meeting went well. It was all about expanding our business into including Solar Energy. I have been working with H&H for over ten years now. It was a medium sized company when I joined and now it has a turnover of over 10 crores. The company builds societies with duplex homes for people. I handle all the marketing & sales for the company. I like my job, it gives me freedom to explore new ideas, an opportunity to integrate those ideas and along with it I get good perks.

I was not happy even after closing a good deal. Vedika's comment that I am selfish was hovering in my mind. I smiled when my bosses congratulated me, I appreciated my colleagues for their hard work. I was doing everything I was supposed to do, still her comment ceased to leave my mind. I went to my office to finish some pending work to take my mind off her but even after working for three hours, her voice was still in my head.

While leaving office I decided to hit the gym before dinner tonight. I was supposed to think about my mom, it was her birthday instead I was thinking about Vedika's comment. Why did it bother me so much, why some girl whom I have never met before, her statement made me so angry? The more I thought about it, the more confused and anxious I got.

Exhausted, I reached home in the nick of time to attend dinner with my family and my soon to be Fiancé Aparna's family. Aparna is the daughter of my father's close friend. We had met quite a few times during family dinners before my father proposed for us to be engaged. I never had a problem as she was well qualified, has a business of her own and was liked by my family that consists of my brother and dad. Hurriedly I got dressed in faded jeans and a polo shirt. It was rude to keep the guests waiting and dad has always believed that.

As soon as I stepped down the stairs the bell rang and there entered Aparna's family, all happy and excited. A part of me missed mom. I always had this thought if mom were alive would she be happy taking Aparna as her daughter-in-law. Mom always believed in love, as my parents' was a love marriage. At that moment I wanted to know what mom would think, there has not been a day gone by when I have not missed her.

Smiling, Aparna came towards and hugged me, with a smile I hugged her back. "Hey, how have you been?" she asked.

"Good" I responded. Satisfied with my answer, she held my hand and we all settled at the dining table. Where dad always celebrated Mom's birthday with family dinners, I liked to spend the day quietly. When it comes to anything related to mom, dad's has always been the final decision, our opinions never mattered. Sometimes it irks me but seeing dad all happy and excited about it, left me with no other option but to follow.

Dinner had all my mom's favourite dishes and I was famished after the intensive workout. I quietly filled my plate and started eating, leaving the entertainment part to my dad. Everyone was laughing, enjoying the dinner and though I was smiling on the outside inside I felt empty. After dinner, everyone settled in the drawing room to enjoy their green tea while I stood near the balcony enjoying the fresh air. Don't take me wrong, I enjoy these occasional family dinners but today I felt a little lost. I have always considered myself to be a modest, honest and caring person but Vedika's statement about me being selfish did not sit well with me at all.

Amidst all the laughter, reminiscing old memories I decided that I need to see Vedika. She needs to know that she shouldn't judge people without knowing them. The moment I decided I felt a little better and then my dad's question, "Ridwan, how about we announce yours and Aparna's engagement next month?" threw me off my balance.

Surprised, I looked at my dad then Aparna, she was blushing, isn't this all happening too soon. I wanted Aparna to look at me and give me some sign, some warning but she was too happy, giggling and excitedly nodding her head in agreement. All eyes were suddenly at me. Shrugging my shoulders, I replied, "Okay that sounds good, if that's what everyone wants." As soon as the words were out of my mouth everyone erupted in congratulating us.

While our families were too excited to call it a night, my mind was too tired to comprehend anything. After few minutes, Aparna came and stood in front of me, a little concerned I asked, "Are you happy with getting engaged next month?"

Aparna answered with a huge smile, "Of course babe, I was waiting for this moment for a long time now."

Nodding, I stared outside, slowly taking breaths to calm the restless feeling I felt. As we were hidden from the others, Aparna came closer towards me and hugged me tightly. I did take my arm around her and tried to feel the warmth she was providing me but nothing helped to calm my restless mind.

3

The Conflict

I got up with a little headache and body ache, dragging myself, I got up to get ready. Generally, it takes me fifteen minutes but today it took me thirty minutes to get ready. Maybe I am catching a flu or something. Dad was sitting at the dining table downstairs, as I entered I went for my cup of coffee straight away.

Folding the newspaper, dad asked, "Is something bothering you?"

Surprised, I replied, "No."

My dad sighed and asked, "Last night you were all quiet, you did not even show any excitement when we announced the engagement."

Looking towards dad, I replied the obvious, "It was mom's birthday and I wanted to spend the day by myself."

Rolling his eyes, he said, "If your mother was alive she would not have wanted her children to sulk on her birthday."

Sipping the coffee, I avoided any eye contact or response. As soon as my coffee was finished, I got up from the table, my dad question stopped in my tracks, "Are you happy Ridwan, I don't want to be a father who imposes everything on his son."

I knew he was trying hard to keep this family close and filling mom's shoes. With a forced smile I turned around and looked into dad's eyes, "Dad marrying Aparna is the right decision, you are not forcing anything."

Reluctantly, he said the words, "But you do not love her?"

Shaking my head, I told him, "Not everyone is as lucky as you and mom."

"I hope you get, one day," he replied. Giving him a smile, I left the house.

I was eager to leave the house, as I wanted to meet Vedika before reaching office. The moment I parked my car in front of the NGO I felt excited and had a tingling sensation which was weird. I was here to give her piece of my mind, so why was I feeling thrilled. Shrugging the feeling, I walked towards the NGO's office and found Sonia sitting at the desk. She saw and greeted me with a warm smile, "Ridwan, so good to see you, how have you been?"

She was the only person after my family who knew how devastated I was after my mother's death. Smiling, I replied, "Good".

Nodding, she accepted my reply and asked, "What brings you here?"

Cautiously, I looked around the office but there was no sign of Vedika, she must be with the elderly people inside. As my eyes came towards Sonia I found her eagerly waiting for my answer, "Umm I think I forgot the receipt yesterday." Of course I thought of an excuse beforehand, I came prepared today.

Shaking her head, she replied, "Vedika is very clumsy sometimes, she must have forgotten to give it to you."

Since she started the topic I carefully enquired, "Where is she?"

Turning around, she asked, "Who?"

"Umm you were talking about Vedika, so I thought I should ask where she is."

"Vedika is busy with her exams, she won't be able to see the NGO for another two weeks." She replied. I nodded and took over the receipt from her.

"By the way, do you know her?' She enquired while writing something in the register.

"Nope, I only met her yesterday." She nodded and kept writing in her register. I stood there for few minutes contemplating whether I should ask her for Vedika's number or address but did not feel right asking her sister. Finally accepting defeat, thanking her, I left the NGO. The whole drive to the office I felt sad that I wouldn't be able to see Vedika again.

It was two weeks later when I went to have lunch in a cafeteria across my office. It was an extremely dull day at the office and treating myself to a good meal would definitely brighten my day. Entering the cafeteria, I took the seat towards a corner, I like my privacy and quietness.

As I was waiting for my order I heard someone yelling. Looking up, I found a girl yelling at the Manager. I surveyed the cafeteria and saw that the only people in the room were the yelling girl group and me.

Since I had nothing better to do I thought of listening in on the conversation.

"It was your fault entirely" the girl yelled. Then the Manager mumbled something to her which I could not hear, to which she replied, "How can you be so rude to your customers?"

Again, the Manager murmured something, and she replied, "I am not going to pay until you give us the correct bill." saying the words she turned towards her group and I could see her face clearly. For a minute I was shocked and a little happy seeing her, my breathing became faster and all I could do was stare at her.

I think my constant staring forced her to look in my direction. The moment she saw me a wide smile erupted on her face and she started walking towards me. I was still in shock. I did not know whether I should keep sitting or should I stand and greet her, my mind stopped working completely. When she came close she greeted, "Ridwan, what a pleasant surprise to meet you here."

She stood in front of my table since I was already late in getting up and I decided to keep sitting. My reply was quite plain in comparison to her cheerful greeting, "Hi Vedika."

Her smile did not falter for a minute. She kept smiling as if she was genuinely happy seeing me and the more she smiled the more uncomfortable I became. Finally, she shifted her attention to the Manager and announced, "Here is my friend, if you have any problem you could come discuss it here."

Without my consent, somehow, she included me in the conversation and before I could even deny, the Manager came up and said politely, "Sir, we have already given them 20% discount on the bill, we do not know what else to do?"

To which Vedika replied, "It isn't about 20%, you should not charge for the dish which we never ate."

Well technically she was right, the Manager should not have charged for the wrong dish but why I was being dragged into this situation was beyond my understanding. Vedika was still arguing with the Manager when I interrupted them, "Can I see the bill?" Manager quietly handed over the bill and pointed out the dish which was not to be entered.

I scanned the dish and the amount and could not believe that this girl was fighting over a dish which amounted to Rs.100 only. The other dishes were much more expensive than the one she ordered. Exasperated with this whole stupid situation I told the Manager, "Are you serious, you are fighting with your customer over Rs.100." The whole situation seemed pointless, I took out a hundred rupee note and asked Vedika to pay the rest of the amount.

Before Vedika could argue, the Manager apologised and assured us that he will remove the said dish. Vedika looked at me with a smile and said, "Wow, Ridwan you are amazing. I have been arguing with him for over 15 minutes and you solved it within a minute."

Shaking my head, I asked, "Do you realise how ridiculous it was to fight over a hundred-rupee dish."

"It was not about the money, it was about principles, that Manager did not have any."

Rolling my eyes, I asked, "Really, where were your principles when you called me selfish?" As soon as the words were out her smile disappeared and she looked at me strangely. I instantly regretted the words, I did not intend to speak it like this, I was about to apologise when she said, "Ridwan, I don't remember calling you that at all." After a few minutes, she sincerely asked, "When did I call you that?"

Something about that truth, about her not remembering the words, not even remembering our meeting irritated me a lot. I have never felt so ignored or invisible like she made me feel. Fuming in anger, I left the restaurant leaving her stunned. A part of me scolded me for behaving like a fifteen-year-old boy but a bigger part of me felt hurt. The thought that I was not that important to her and that she did not even remember what she said to me was disturbing. Is it her or am I not that important to anyone in my life. Anxious, I called Aparna, she picked up the phone on the second call, "Yes Ridwan, what's the hurry?" she asked.

A little disoriented with my thoughts, I took time to speak and finally overcoming my embarrassment, I asked, "Do you miss me?"

"What, your voice is cracking, could you speak again?"

Breathing in, I asked again stressing on each word, "Aparna, do you miss me?'

"Really Ridwan, you called to ask me this?" she asked, a little irritated.

"Why can't I call my fiancé to ask this?" I asked in an irritated tone.

I could hear her taking deep breaths before she answered, "Ridwan, I am in the middle of an important meeting. Can I call you later on this?"

It broke my heart to hear her response, how much time does it take to answer a simple question. Shouldn't she be missing me? After all we are going to get engaged soon. Am I only means to an end. As soon as this thought came into my mind I shut it down. Aparna was a successful entrepreneur and she does not need me or my money, she was an accomplished woman who can take care of herself. Brushing these thoughts away, I called my friend Ansh. Thankfully he picked up on the second ring. As soon as he did I asked him, "do you miss me?'

I could hear the surprise when he asked, "What's wrong, bro?"

"There is nothing wrong. I asked you a simple question: do you miss me?"

"Bro, where are you?" Ansh asked.

"In my office, why?"

"Okay, you wait there. I have a meeting to attend in ten minutes which will be over in fifteen minutes. Then let me come to your office, we will talk."

Rolling my eyes, I replied, "Ansh I am okay, no need to come here." Still he insisted and told me he will be there in an hour.

What is wrong with everyone? A simple yes or no question and they are taking so much time to answer. Have I seriously not been missed by anyone? The thought is annoying and tiresome. Every time I meet Vedika, the after effects are not good. Every time she forces me to question things about me and my life. I start doubting myself and people close to me. Why the hell does she have this effect on me? I need to stop this madness. I need to make sure she does not bother me in any way. I need to meet her and sort this out once and for all.

4
The Argument

Generally, I spent my weekends relaxing or with my family or finish some pending work or meetings. But this Saturday, it seems impossible to relax or stop the thoughts from troubling me. Turning over, I picked up my laptop and searched about the NGO online where I found a few clippings and Sonia's photograph but there was no website. I typed Vedika's name on the search engine but nothing related to her popped up. How am I supposed to find her when I do not have her address or phone number? As Sonia already mentioned she won't be visiting the NGO, how on earth am I going to find her?

Suddenly it struck me, opening my social media I started searching for her. Since I did not know her surname as Sonia had a different one that left me with only one option- to use different tags along with her name to find her. After half an hour of searching I finally found her page. Browsing through her page I was surprised to see that her profile revealed everything about her life, from her birthday to phone number to address. How careless can she be?

The more I browsed her profile the angrier I got, everything about her life was on display. I also think she was addicted to social media as there was some kind of update on her profile every three hours. I did not think this girl could be any more transparent than her profile page. Noting her number on my mobile, I thought of leaving her a message but however hard I tried I could not think of a reasonable reply.

I thought it would be better if I meet in person and speak to her. Quickly I took a screenshot of her address and got up to get ready to visit her home. I have no clue how she would react on seeing me or would it look stalkerish if I visit her home? I kept on justifying my reasons to visit her home by saying it was openly shared on her profile so not my fault if I drop by.

I had a few questions in my mind and I kept repeating them in my head while driving to her home. It took me an hour to reach her home due to the weekend rush on the roads and on top of that it was drizzling too. The moment I reached her society, it took me several minutes to locate her house as it was the last house in the society and it was surrounded with greenery and flowers. I hesitated for a few minutes before getting out. I knew my questions would sound funny to her or may appear desperate but I needed answers. I needed to speak to her, needed some clarity.

I rang the house bell five times before she opened the door. She looked radiant and shocked. It was good to see her silent and shocked for a change, otherwise she never knew how to stop talking. Seeing her like this brought a different kind of relief to my senses and a smile. My smile got her back from the dazed stupor as she asked, "Ridwan, oh my my! so you know how to smile too."

Leave it to her, no hi or hello, direct attack on me. I felt embarrassed for a minute and then composing myself I greeted her, "Hi Vedika."

Smiling, she responded, "Hello Ridwan, so nice to see you." She felt nice seeing me. That warmed my heart a little bit.

That uncomfortable feeling whenever I was around her settled, I asked, "Can I come in?"

Scrunching her face, she replied, "Sorry, please do." It was a small house compared to others in the society and as we reached the drawing room I was shocked by the mess it was in. There were sketches all around the floor and table, few pencils were on the floor, there were too many files scattered on the sofa. How she could live in such a mess was beyond me. I looked towards her while eyeing the place, smiling sheepishly she removed a few files from the chair and patted on the chair for me to sit.

Shaking my head, I walked towards that chair. While finding a place for herself to sit she asked, "So what brings you here?"

It took me a minute to recollect my reason to visit. I did not want to directly ask her instead I started, "Do you realise that your social media has everything about you on public display."

She replied in a confused tone, "Yes."

Glaring at her, I continued, "Do you know how dangerous it is, anyone could misuse that information, could follow you home or I don't know, it is not right to have your address and number displayed on social media."

"Okay" her face was expressionless.

Her one word replies and blank expression made me mad, I continued, "Vedika, I never pegged a person as aware as you to be so dumb."

That comment brought back the colour on her face and she asked, "Why were you looking at my social profile?"

I had an answer in my head for this but it did not sound good enough to speak out loud. I was still formulating an answer when she spoke again, "You know, I would call this stalking." I looked up to see if she was joking and was surprised to see she was not.

Straightening, I stood up and told her, "I was not stalking, I wanted to meet you so I looked you up."

"Well, technically that is called stalking."

Narrowing my eyes, I lashed out, "that's what you are good at, judging and fighting with people. You judged me that I was selfish and then conveniently forgot about it. Then you picked up a fight with the manager and now you are unnecessarily picking a fight with me. For the past few days you have been messing with my head, forcing me to feel things that I am not ready to face yet." It felt like I was on a roll, "I have repeatedly told myself that things you think about me or say should not make any difference to me but they do and that is infuriating. You are such a mess, look at your house, everything is so scattered and messy. Whenever I meet you..."

I could not finish the line as she interrupted in between, "Why are you here, Ridwan?"

"To tell you that I am not selfish and that you cannot make me feel invisible." She was totally opposite of me, while I was writhing in anger she was calm and composed.

She calmly asked, "Why does it bother you so much what I think?"

Irritated, I spoke, "I don't know and I am engaged, so it shouldn't." It was more of a statement than question.

"Yes it shouldn't and I also think you should leave, Ridwan, I have a paper to prepare for and honestly I do not understand the reason for your visit." She did it again, dismissed me as easily as before. It never mattered to her how she behaved with me. Feeling insulted and hurt, I left her house and banged the door loudly before leaving. It was then and there in my car outside her house that I decided I would never talk or meet her again.

5

The Questions

Later that evening, I had dinner plans with Aparna at 8 pm. I decided that I should focus more on my fiancé than Vedika. Vedika was a mistake or an interlude in my life which happened because I got over emotional due to Mom's birthday week. It was a chain reaction to a lot of things happening in my life. It was 6:30 already, and getting up from bed I got ready before I was late for dinner.

An hour later, I was waiting outside Aparna's house to pick her up. She was looking beautiful in a green dress but my heart did not flutter and I did not feel even a fraction of the excitement I felt when I was with Vedika. I stopped mentally comparing the two and focused on Aparna. I complimented her and she look surprised. On asking she replied, "it is the first time you ever complimented me, babe." apologising for being so insensitive, I started driving towards the restaurant.

We were listening to some song when my mind drifted again. I had no idea why my thoughts kept returning to Vedika. Aparna was smart, beautiful, the way she carried herself was very elegant and she was not at all messy. She was perfect in every sense. Then why was I not attracted to her, why did I not feel the spark like I feel when I am around Vedika. I was a riot of emotions when I was with Vedika but with Aparna I did not feel anything similar.

The dinner went on fine. We spoke about her business plans, my new project and about engagement clothes. I avoided talking about the engagement day as much as I could because the moment that topic came up I started feeling that uncomfortable feeling again. Finally, the dinner was over and I dropped Aparna back home. This whole dinner thing with Aparna should make me feel good and excited about us but it felt more like my duty. Blaming it all on Vedika, I retired to my bed and promised not to think about her or ever see her again.

The whole week went away in a blur as I was swamped with work and meetings. I kept on getting calls from Aparna to finalise the appointment with her designer but I kept avoiding it. The closer the engagement day got the more I felt like avoiding my family and Aparna. I checked my mobile and there was another reminder from Aparna, I felt guilty for avoiding her. Sighing, I messaged her back to schedule the appointment for the day after tomorrow. I got a thumbs up in response and I put my mobile aside.

Opening my laptop, I directly went to Vedika's social media profile. Yes, I have been keeping tabs on her through her profile. I tried avoiding her but I could not stop thinking about her so to quieten my mind I started visiting her profile daily, only for few minutes though. I noticed there have been no updates on her profile for past two days and that worried me a bit more than it was necessary. I thought of dropping her a message but that would seem stalkerish to her. If she does not update in another two hours then I would give her a call.

Swamped with work, I did not realise it had been three hours since I last took a break. Sighing and closing the last file, I opened her profile page and scrolled down, still there was no update from her side. I tensed up as she was not the type of person who would go without updating at least once in the whole day. Forgetting all about my ego I dialled her number. Once, twice, thrice, I called her at least five times and every time it went to her voicemail. My heart started beating faster and palms got sweaty, the thought of something bad happening to her was scary.

I looked outside my office window and it was raining heavily. Instantly my mind started conjuring up scenes with the worst possibilities. Scared, I got up and started running towards my car all the while consoling myself that she would be safe at home. It took me forty-five minutes to reach her house, running in the rain I reached outside the door and rang the bell. I kept ringing the bell for another fifteen minutes but there was no response. Terror which was only a possibility now turned into a reality. I tried her number again but she never picked up.

Sitting back in my car, I thought of checking at the NGO, which was my last hope before I would totally lose it. The drive to the NGO was slow due to the traffic and it took every effort for me to not go into panic mode. The moment I reached the NGO I left my car in a haphazard way and ran inside. Breathless, I reached the main office and opened the door. As I entered I found the table stacked up with files and a few papers on the floor. I found her standing next to the cupboard, taking some files out. The relief which washed over me was unexplainable. For a few minutes I just stood there watching her, it felt normal doing that. As I kept watching her my heart beat became normal and that uncomfortable feeling which I always felt when I am not near her seemed to ease down.

Vedika turned around and yelped as soon as she saw me. The files in her hand fell down, "What the hell Ridwan, you scared the shit out of me."

Narrowing my gaze, I replied," I scared the shit out of you, you did that, for the last two days there have been no updates on your profile then you haven't been picking up my phone. This was the only place left to check up on you. Do you realise how scary it is to not know where you were?"

In between my rants she went towards the desk, removed a few files and picked up her mobile. Opening the phone her one eye brow went up, that must be the missed calls I left on her mobile. When I finished she explained, "Phone was silent, I had exams these past two days. So, I have been busy with the exams and then I had to sort these files which were pending since past two weeks. I got immersed in that and forgot about time."

Her explanation brought another wave of relief but she was looking at me differently. I had to ask, "What?"

Sighing, she walked towards me and asked, "Ridwan what are you doing here, you are engaged, why are behaving like this?"

Getting offended by her questions, I replied, "I got scared, so thought of checking up on you. What's wrong in this?"

Smiling sadly, she asked, "Do you check your fiancé's profile too? Do you get scared when she is not around? Do you find her the way you found me? Aren't you supposed to do all this for her instead of me?"

These were valid questions but I did not have answers to any of them. Slumping my shoulders I answered honestly, "I don't know."

"Then I think you should call or meet me only when you have the answers. Please Ridwan, I am really grateful for your concern but you have to leave." Somehow, it made sense and I did not have the energy to fight her or get angry at her for throwing me out again. Nodding, I turned around and left, taking that uncomfortable feeling with me again.

6

The Acceptance

I was confused and lost, nothing excites me about today. Today is the day when I get engaged to Aparna. Past few days have been like a roller coaster ride with her, I realised that a lot of things about us did not match. She wanted a huge gala affair where I wanted a simple engagement, she wanted us to colour co-ordinate and I hated these type of things. Last night when she was stressed about her outfit, for a minute I felt like telling her we should rethink this whole engagement thing but then her mother came and I did not have the courage to say it out loud.

Two days before, I told my friend Ansh, about my feelings for Vedika and how I feel that this engagement with Aparna was not the right thing to do. Honestly, it freaked him out more than me accepting my feelings. His advice was to let this engagement happen and later we would figure things out. Somehow, my heart could not agree to this solution. I felt like I was cheating on my family and Aparna by lying to them. I am supposed to leave the house in half an hour to check up on decorations in the hotel but before that I wanted to speak to my dad.

Stepping down, I saw Ansh sitting with dad. I casually walked towards them. Ansh was supposed to meet us directly at the venue. Lifting my eyebrows, I looked at him which he absolutely ignored. I was about to speak to dad when Ansh said, "Uncle, I am taking Ridwan along with me, we will meet you all directly at the venue."

Ignoring him, I spoke. "Dad, I wanted to speak to you."

Ansh again interrupted, "You can speak to Uncle later, we have to leave now." Saying this, he dragged me out of the house.

Once outside, I shouted at him, "What the hell bro."

He calmly replied, "You will thank me later." After that I refused to speak to him. It was at that moment, it became clear that this engagement was the wrong decision. It was irritating to see Ansh hovering around me until it was time to get ready for the function. While we were getting ready Ansh got a call from my dad. Though he tried to convince my dad to let someone else take the responsibility but dad was dad and once he has decided no one can change his mind.

I always hated this habit of dad's but today I was thankful for him. As soon as Ansh left I threw my outfit on the bed, wore my jeans and shirt, and left the room. Believe me, I was feeling guilty for abandoning my family and Aparna at the last minute but getting engaged was not an option. I knew this was all too drastic and things could be sorted out easily if only I had a chance to speak to my dad. Now it was too late for any kind of discussion and leaving the party was the only solution.

As I reached the hotel exit I saw Aparna's family coming out of the car. Afraid they might see me, I took the umbrella lying next to the door and hiding myself from them I left the hotel on foot. It was raining heavily, I kept on walking for a long time before I found a secluded bench and sat over it.

I kept getting calls from Ansh and messages too but I ignored it all. Sighing I messaged dad, "Sorry dad, I cannot get engaged to Aparna. I know it's too late but she is not the one."

Then I called her, the only person whose voice would calm me and her reply would help sort this mess out. For a change, she picked up on the second ring, on her hello I replied, "I know the answer, I have fallen in love with you Vedika."

There was silence for few minutes so I thought she disconnected, I was about to check when I heard her saying, "It's crazy, stupid and foolish to admit but I have fallen for you too, Ridwan".

About Shradha Khanna

An MBA in International Business, Shradha has multifarious talents. After working with her family firm, she ventured into speciality baking. Being a trend setter and breaking traditional barriers by opening the first eggless bakery owned and managed by a women entrepreneur in Agra. Blessed by his Holiness Sri Sri Ravi Shankar, Shradha is humbled and honoured to be a member of the Art of Living family which gives her a platform to further unleash her creative talents and abilities and share them forward to bring a smile on others face. Encouraged by her mother, to pen her thoughts soon saw her seeing her first novel 'Should I Fall in Love' with Rigi Publications in bookstores in 2016, her second novel 'The Emotional Connection' with Juggernaut books on their app in 2018 and her third novel What Went Wrong came out in 2021 from Kalamos Literary Services LLP.

9 789390 909063